Boy in a Boat

ROY BENTLEY

Boy in a Boat

1/26/88

To Bob,

In friendship..

All best wishes —

Roy

The University of Alabama Press

Copyright © 1986 by
The University of Alabama Press
University, Alabama 35486–2877
All rights reserved
Manufactured in the United States of America

Library of Congress Cataloging-in-Publication Data

Bentley, Roy, 1954–
  Boy in a boat.

  (Alabama poetry series)
  I. Title.   II. Series.
PS3552.E564B6   1986   811'.54   85-24508
ISBN 0-8173-0290-5 (alk. paper)
ISBN 0-8173-0291-3 (pbk. : alk. paper)

For Sherry

ACKNOWLEDGMENTS

Some of the poems in this collection appeared originally in the following publications:

The Bellingham Review
In Praise of That Same Motion; The Young American Wrestles His First Harley-Davidson

Centered on Columbus
The Fire in Earnest

The Chariton Review
White Handkerchief; 33 South; On the Failure of All Political Poems

Farmer's Market
The Man Who Digs for Fish (*as* Boy in a Boat)

Four Quarters
Shirts; Christmas, Coffman's Farm; Certain Flowers Persist

Gambit
The L & K Plays Host to the Class of '72

The Indiana Review
Ralph Waldo Emerson Addresses the ICBM Silos at Minot, North Dakota

Intro
1953

Light They're After
Night Fishing the Ohio; The Importance of Singing Before Long Silence

The Ohio Journal
North-South; Turning Thirty the Year Orwell Made Famous

The OHIO REVIEW
On the Diamond Behind Garfield Elementary, Melvin White Proves There Is but One Boog Powell; The Heart as Second Child

Passion For Industry
White Church October; Why Mark Chapman Got Both Legs of His Good Pants Wet; Mario Soto Drops His Head in Disappointment as George Hendrick Circles the Bases

Poetry Ohio
In Ohio We Celebrate As Best We Can

Pudding
Blue Pony Rag; The Way into Town (*as* Whitesburg)

riverSedge
Barracks; For Matthew

Ship of Fools
The New Air Force Tucks Itself in Minutes from the Alamo

A portion of this collection appeared previously as the chapbook *The Way into Town* (Signpost Press).

Contents

ix

III

Who serves Virtue works alone, unaided, in a chilly vacuum of reserved judgment; where, pledge yourself to Non-virtue and the whole countryside boils with volunteers to help you.
— William Faulkner, *The Reivers*

The first thing to see, looking away over the water, was a kind of dull line—that was the woods on t'other side—you couldn't make nothing else out; then a pale place in the sky; then more paleness, spreading around; then the river softened up, away off, and warn't black any more, but gray; you could see little dark spots drifting along, ever so far away— trading scows, and such things; and long black streaks— rafts; sometimes you could hear a sweep screaking; or jumbled up voices, it was so still, and sounds come so far.
— Mark Twain, *Huckleberry Finn*

I

1953

1
In Fleming, Kentucky, the hills rise up.
Walking the ridge, gathering blackberries,
she hears a rasp of crickets, yap of dogs
chasing children in the dust.
Down the hollow near where she lives
wet horses walk through shoulder-high corn,
leaves parting to let them pass.

2
Back from Ashland Pen her husband has his
picture taken on the fender of a '46 Chevy truck;
sees on the sidewalk in front of the drugstore
Junior Tucker who helped sell the whiskey
that got him a year. As if it would buy it all back
he catches Tuck with one good right, then a left.

There is nothing hurried in the way he says it —
"That son-of-a-bitch shot me" —
and walks the block or so to Fleming Hospital.
There, quiet, kidding with a nurse he'd
gone to school with,
hole in his liver the size of a dime:
Go tell Mary.

3

3

"Live long enough and you bury 'em all," she says,
staring at the 8 × 10, thin man
leaning forward into gray.
All those years, his children,
tying first shoes,
to bury him on the hill above Goose Creek
in the rain —
casket into flat bed, road straight up,
slipping in clay, catching herself,
truck chain stretched tight, holding this once.

4

Christmas, Coffman's Farm

North corner of the near field,
abandoned grain barn, Ford tractor on blocks.
Nearer the house by a cistern, three
snowmen it took ladders to finish,
biggest with a smile half its face.
Across the yard, in porchlight,

cats claw each other for a half-plate of chicken,
snow flying the few minutes it takes
the big Gray to win out.
Year-old child presses against door glass,
claps his hands. In the kitchen
his mother to a man next to her:
"Told you they's hungry."

Last of the sun warm on the door
cat comes quiet to the porch, raises itself
even with the child. At the glass small mouths open.
Steam catches the sound.

Off State Route 79, Nettie Potter Bentley Comes Clean about the Middle Class

The most profound thing my mother ever said
was that life, most days,
is neither black nor white but a bland gray.
We look out the window any chill uncloudy day
and wish it warmer, wish ourselves in Challis, Idaho,
where "everyone wears spurs—
even the women, even to bed."
The whole gray story begins around us:
as always at evening the cows come,
pairs of men break and scatter bales,
blind Collie wanders from a hill of late hay
onto the eave of a barn roof.

Small towns like this, dark air owns the body.
What is done, once started,
blazes and burns low,
car or truck lights fire enough this far in.
Near end of a big pole barn—leaning, one side
still selling tobacco—woman fast-sweeps a walk,
tells a neighbor, "When Frank Sinatra died
in Montgomery Clift's arms in *From Here to Eternity,*
you knew there was no justice."
Above, old dog,
backward stepping, jumps, lands yelping in a shrub.

Night Fishing the Ohio

He knows something, this old shovelhead.
Close in, like good whiskey,
he has the blood believing again.
Yet a part of him needs the hook,
its pull into light to keep going.
The Masonic Lodge of Belpre, Ohio, would agree.
On the near bank, two of their number
brace a weight of wood and oxbone,
carry it stumbling, sidestepping an old dog.

In a clearing by lantern light,
every full belly recalls the flesh,
takes its turn, hefts ax and sledge,
breaks the ribs, spine,
legs stripped now of all that muscle.
I feel each hard blow ring
at the bait-end of twelve-pound test.
Bone bits spray outward in the dark.
Upstream, deer lean across and into barbed wire,
the apples there worth a little blood.

White Handkerchief

1
The first time I had my fortune told
was by a woman who taught English
at a technical school.
Had a black belt in judo.
Pick a card, she said and played a tape
of Peter, Paul, and Mary.

I pointed to the King of Cups.
Cut them, she said.
How much I believed of what she said
is hard to say.
In a way I believed it all.
When she was finished,
I gave her a ride into Nelsonville, dropped her
at a Sohio station as if magic belonged there.
She drove away in a jeep.

2
On a small rise the third week of spring,
walking,
I notice at the edge of a leaf in wind
a moment in which the underside
is seen clearly, when rise and fall
are one motion, connection tenuous as rain.

Legs are stiff with going up.
I see that turning repeated, recall the night
Tom Kozlowski spoke in tongues
in a basement in Newark, Ohio.
Tom rocking, chanting,
I heard what I took to be God,
afterwards, asked how much was his.
Shrugging, Tom smiled: *You tell me.*

3
When I was thirteen, Virgil Horsley
stood at the front of the Heath Baptist Church,
white handkerchief in his cupped hand,
and in the lightest Southern accent I have ever heard
told me I was lost. My grandmother
who read to me from a big King James—
"and the blood came trickling down"—
would have been proud as I went forward,
tears streaming
all the way to nineteen when I cut my wrist
and saw bright and gray in the meat
how stupid it would be to waste this.

Now, in the middle distance,
I hear Virgil Horsley too is lost—
shipped out on a tanker, drunk,
ranting there is no God.
Suddenly the weather changes
and he is part of whatever it means
to say something is past protecting.

On dry land it is easy to separate out
the brick church by Ramp Creek, dull voice
that pleaded its way through 1967:
One more verse. While we wait.

9

33 South

In fall in Athens County, truck exhaust
mixes with the scent of wild onions;
busloads of students hang from windows,
toss pop bottles in high arcs at roadsigns.

As the bus turns I catch sight of one
blond sixteen-year-old, imagine
Sunday at the Midland, buttered popcorn
between us, holding hands,
John Wayne to an Indian, "That's far enough."
Then slowly the feel of hand becomes breast, thigh,

billboard for a Baptist church,
holes in it,
verse reading *I am,*
hillside, ash branches filling in
the Way, the Truth and the Life.

In Ohio We Celebrate As Best We Can

1

Over the highest hill in Kettering, Ohio,
Beth and Wes Vines run
into fields of day lily and Queen Anne's lace,
the test always who can play at dying
well enough—best one dead, first one up.
Master of the Quick Death,
Wes can drop from any low tree
the way he sees gray television Germans do
under Vic Morrow's righteous Thompson sub.

Actually, they play in a junkyard.
What wildflowers there are
grow through truck parts, old Hotpoint stoves.
The orchard that borders
is full of Winesap and June apples.

When they have had enough of counterfeiting death,
they build a tunnel under the junk,
digging and hauling out wagonfuls of cool earth,
shoring up ceiling and wall with crate wood
taken from the orchard first thing each morning.
When the tunnel is finished and wide enough
they play there until the roof falls,
then, buried to the neck, squirm
like cicadas
blind-digging hard Ohio to smell a junkyard.

11

2
First day of deer season, old Chevy
smokes up 33 South, eight-point buck
tied to the trunk.
At every bump, body rises,
drops back, rain freezing on the eyes.

Outside Nelsonville, a wire breaks.
Forelegs and head drop, drag behind in the dark.
Taillights blaze.
A door slams. Another.
Two men stand in moonlight,
pass a pint of whiskey once before lifting.

3
I can still smell Jody McLaughlin's perfume
as we danced in the union hall on Hudson Avenue,
ten years from high school.
Beside us, Dave Hanley—married, one boy—
leaned into Sherri Link.
He had wanted her since we were freshmen.

In near dark they moved,
Jody telling me of a job she was glad to have
what with Reagan
and half that small town looking for work.

As we danced and talked
I thought of the only girl in tenth grade
who would kiss me on a dare.
In the hall after history class
she gave me reason to stand perfectly still.
Any movement and I would begin forgetting.

4

On a low hill, a tire swing
turns from the last and lowest branch of a maple.
Blond boy, facedown,
sees the earth blur before him,
the turning already an old friend.
In the house down the hill
his grandmother bakes gingerbread, calls his name —
her thin voice, the short ROWEE.
Where he is, rope tightens,
the noise it makes a kind of singing
like the hinge of a door.
Above all this, he hears and is wiggling
from the old 2-ply tire to the crest of the hill,
calling up the taste of her hot ponebread —
wet, soaking with butter.
Over the top he yells to her,
prepares to feel her apron, each sticky-sweet stain.

5

Off to the side of the road in and out
of Carbon Hill, Ohio,
there is a place just wide enough for a '68 Chevy.
First warm day in March,
I sit eating apricots and bread,
discussing death with a woman who sees it
as the thing pressing even blood forward.
Crumbs collect in her lap as she talks.
Outside, a great quiet
collides with the notion it is somehow important
to make noisy sense.
Brushing herself, she hands back the apricots.
Cows, wintered down the hollow,
call as coal trucks slow
and shift for the tight turn into Carbon Hill.

White Church October

Everything is going to have to be put back.
— W. S. Merwin

1
All afternoon we make a game
of clearing old apples from the yard,
tossing them for hours at a break in the fence.
Bill Potter, our uncle, has the arm for this, bets us
he can hit five-for-five and does.
Near dusk, finished for the day,
he takes us to the drugstore, buys fountain Cokes.
When we were younger — October leaf forts,
his mother's yard — he took movies of us.
The Christmas we saw them,
he ran them backward: all the leaves
poured into place.
Those we had thrown skyward
held, fell then gently to hand.

2
Toward the river he takes us,
over and through fence, across fields wet still
from the rain of the night before.
At last on the bank, cousins settling in —
strong wind, quail, and cricket.
"Gonna bite like hell," Bill says.
He hands us each a roll, laughs.
No one washes between bait and breakfast.

First fish of the day, small channel cat,
he shows us to reach around spines
that rise between rough fingers.
He feeds the hook backward through torn mouth,
rubs the smooth underskin: "This one
gonna have babies."
And in a low arc throws it back.

3
The summer of the biopsy,
he builds a Pentecostal church in Louisville.
He can do anything with wood—
dollhouse rocking chairs from clothespin halves,
cattle barns not a quarter inch off square.

After the cancer, we bring him to a hill
outside Shepherdsville, Kentucky.
Twin white churches beyond a field.
Were he to see this, he would note
the facts of wood fifty, a hundred years old:
seal of window frame, depth of wall,
the kind of paint.
Bad dovetailing on that tongue-and-groove.

4
The body deserts us. But not tonight.
Tonight, thousands of insects
sing in Johnson grass and cocklebur.
I know better than to say they sing for Bill Potter.
I say it anyway.
It sounds like throwing something back.

15

Why Mark Chapman Got Both Legs
of His Good Pants Wet

It was 1970, my first poem,
and I read in a high school restroom, Mark Chapman
laughing so hard he fell, cussing,
into a half-wall urinal.
The handful who gathered to help him up
marveled either at the power of the spoken word
or the spectacle. After, in biology,
boat-shaped mitochondria steered blind,
lanky chromosomes bent like fishermen
leaning into more than they could land.

On the Tennessee River that year
we fished with ropes the warmer water
below TVA dams,
whole small bluegill as bait,
bank-end of the rope staked deep
because a 40-pound catfish tears arms free
if it hits right.
What hook and rope accomplished below the dams,
I wanted done in that restroom.
Never mind that mad, high laugh
as if what I was doing was slapstick,
Fields or Chaplin. It was a dark year.
The clear things were fish and dividing cells—
furrows in cytoplasm stained visible and dead,
shovelhead big and slick as the floor
that met Mark Chapman.

16

The last class of the day was history.
Had it been 1770, men like Simon Kenton —
six days naked in winter, Shawnee
near enough to touch —
I might have written of a land called *Can-tuc-kee,*
game plentiful and God so present
he rated two names.
Might have written of the gauntlet,
Shawnee method of testing courage — two lines,
club and tomahawk blows on a common lane.
The trick then was not to stop, to shout
either of God's names and run with every cell
straining to light. Almost no one made it.
You knew that when you ran.

17

The Way into Town

By the railroad bridge, a mile out,
Brud Lequire and I count boxcars.
After thirty-two, thirty-three,
the train begins slowing.
In the few seconds it is stopped
we rush from bikes, crawl between wheels,
a beating in our ears loud and sure as the rail.

Train past, we pick up air rifles,
pepper crows, cats, anything that moves.
Brud suggests we ride through Whitesburg
to the barber shop, read comics Granville leaves
Saturdays by the shoeshine box.

Big four-blade fan spinning above,
Granville dusts a customer,
scent of talc filling the long room.
Cash register, bell on the door—
Brud traces with worn shoes
circles in piles of hair near the shinebox.

Two to go, Granville takes a break,
buys us RC's,
says there's a month left of summer
and his roof leaks.
He offers to let us each earn a dollar spreading tar:
"Four movies in a dollar."
Later, by the bridge, we plan,
hear suddenly the whistle and begin counting.

The Man Who Digs for Fish

for Keith Rhodes

1. *Boy in a Boat*

Striking the surface, he works his small net—
hand over hand, close to the body—
takes from its hollow enough to feed this day,
then throws bread, days old,
dust on the lake,
makes them come again—
two's and three's,
drawn to whatever movement divides whole light.
Each time, over and over,
he strikes, finds the net,
bread, until he has all he can
hope for, all he can carry
without waste. Tonight,
in a room warm with fire
he will feel this repetition,
find, in every muscle, something of the fish.

2. The Man Who Digs for Fish

A path of least resistance brings them —
rock bass, Chinook, rainbow — downstream,
too close to shallows. In an inch of air,
breathing sand and silt,
they swallow, eyes large and open.
From the drier places he frees them,
gulls high above, turning spirals
as here, each fights,
dives fast and deep to darker water.
For trapped fish it is enough: one man,
fingers calloused by fins.
Enough that it begin with the touch,
the lifting up out of this body.

In Praise of That Same Motion

for Scott Minar

The night Ed Laurenzo ran a kickoff back 87 yards,
slipping six tackles, I sat beside
Sandy Langford at Newark High Stadium.
Eddie was so smooth, falling
forward the last few feet to score.
And after the game,
backseat of my mother's Ford,
stretched out, windows steamed from our breath,
we came so close.
At the last minute she sat up, wiped a window
to see out.

Years later, in her backyard,
I remember her telling me not to marry.
There, in the heat of summer, August,
I told her I wouldn't, then,
calling up names of men she liked as well,
sent her an invitation, next day in the mail.

There is a part of us that longs to move
like Eddie Laurenzo, ever forward,
freeing ourselves. And if we can dream but once
we have the ball, game dead even,
see a hole the size of Cleveland, and falling,
spinning, finding the mark
make it 22–16, why not?

North-South

1
In Kettering, Ohio, I am eleven, almost twelve.
Shelly Staddon, tall and dark,
comes to 6th grade waving *Meet the Beatles*
as if an album can erase the fact she is
months from a bra.
"No more horses at recess," she says.
Though I cannot name them, even at eleven I know
there are opposites reached for:
the north-south of us
is that we want it all, innocence
and the good feel of those we collide with at play.
If the world is Kettering, Ohio,
I shout for Shelly Staddon to rest like she did
on the ledge of my thigh at dance practice.
We were partners.
I remember how light she was, how warm
in that one spot.
I think of this when she comes in,
love songs handheld above her,
how it will be a long time before she forgets
and smiles my way at the coatrack
where once when she said the word *stallion*
I knew exactly what it meant.

2
The summer I was sixteen, there was a lounge chair.
Green-white webbing, cheap thin steel.
A girl whose neck I kissed on a whim:
"Gives me chill bumps," she said. "Do it again."
All summer, we tried to fit two into the chair,
small tears in the webbing complaining as we moved.

Behind her house was a field, open all the way
to the air base where our fathers worked.
First week of August, the corn in the field
was just high enough to hide us.
When the chair broke,
we took a blanket to a place we could find at night.
She was to climb from her window
to the limb of a maple, drop down
quiet as a cat, we hoped.
I waited that night for the sound of her landing.
Next morning she reminded me she was fifteen,
told me not to tell her I loved her:
I gotta go back in.

3
These days, summer is a 24-hour sign
humming *Liquor Store* through a window at noon.
Lottery line at the carryout below
reaching for that long-shot million or two.
Even the slight, dark man
who takes the money until his fingers hurt
believes if not this time, the next.
The woman who spends half her monthly check:
"Buy bread, you got bread. Some bread,
some numbers," she says,
"you got hope."

Across fence, it is 3rd and 1.
Hard young men collide claiming three forward feet.

23

On the Diamond Behind Garfield Elementary, Melvin White Proves There Is but One Boog Powell

When Dave Wheeler fielded the hard one-hopper
to short, he fired the ball to Melvin White,
forgetting the huge first baseman
moved like molasses.
Melvin caught it on his sternum.
You could hear the breath escaping
all the way to center field.

Falling in love is like that,
begging air as the infield laughs hysterically.
You could be dying, blue and big as Melvin White.
It could be spring and the woman married.
She could be dark
and fine as air the hour after rain.
Still, they would double over laughing,
the pain getting worse.

And after she had gone,
you would catch her scent, imagine
strong small hands halving apricots
as you fall face first, runner advancing.
Of course, eventually the pain would ease.
You would stand.
It would be important that the game go on.
You would recall a score,
how far behind you were when it hit,
only this bright burning in the lungs.

The Return of Ballroom Dancing

The joke was that Sumner, Illinois, was the size
of a good ballroom — one flashing yellow light,
nothing to impede the movement through.
Willard Jones said it, told Leonard Holmes —
his friend on the B & O — who told his uncle
at the Rotary in Claremont, who told everyone
at the ice plant, slapped his side, and started
the comparison back around toward Sumner.
When the joke returned and circulated,
Willard knew exactly who'd started it.
Especially since ballroom dancing hadn't been
anywhere near Sumner in close to thirty years.

The last time Willard danced, it was with Garnett
his wife. She wasn't his wife then and didn't
drink like she did after they married.
Garnett in taffeta and perfume, Willard in black tie:
he liked to think of the dancing, not
pulling the tires from Garnett's Ford to keep her
from buying whiskey, her driving it on the rims,
long miles in a hard rain. Tonight he's forgetting,
taking Ruth Butterfield byGod
to the Red Hills State Park
to kiss and whatever else in the pine needles.
(He'd take her to his house, but Garnett's only been
dead a year and people would talk.)

They talk anyway. Like now
as he moves through the wood door
of Pauline Piper's drugstore,
half the Odd Fellows Lodge turning
then slowly back, Orris Brown's entire family
making that low clicking noise with the tongue and
teeth, bells of the Central Christian down the street
ringing nine times clear, thin-waisted Ruth Butterfield
sliding across her side of the booth, big-smiling
at Willard like they've already been to Red Hills.

II

The Young American Wrestles His First Harley-Davidson

for Billy Barnett

"Clutch stuck," you told us
and pushed the black '48 panhead
up the embankment.
Mounted again.
Rode with a curse for God on your lips.
Same curse set free at fifteen
stealing the tin roof from Frances Potter's barn,
selling the metal. Five dollars, a month of Marlboros.

What was it about you nothing could conquer?
The good looks? The way you shot straight pool?
The time you put a diamondback in the glove box
of your truck, made Dolores your sister
listen to the rattle and hiss
the four and three-quarter miles
down Pound Mountain? Try anything once.

Today, it is 1961. June.
The foot clutch has slipped, and you smile
as the big bike hook-slides you and it
under my father's truck.
A last red-lettered flash: *Roy's Shell. AX 8-9381.*
Tall, thin Ronnie Hall laughing, choking hard
on a Coca-Cola.

Eight years and you will lean over a shotgun.
Send that James Dean myth and one blue eye
into the wall.
This minute though, Billy, you're a hero.
A minor god I trade shirts with.

Shirts

The shirt I slept in is wrinkled now. It lies beside
my bed, quiet — a squirrel I buried one Christmas.
Both sleeves, still rolled, cross like pages of the paper
we used as shroud. The shirt is brown. I have
seven the same: I am reminding myself that each day

is a dream I wear, walk in
till something strips me. It is hard to dream.

Six shirts hang in the closet. The one she bought
that Christmas, lost; one among many
I may have worn it
today. I cannot know. Six sets of arms stand as one
in shadow, edges smoothed in. I count them.
Tomorrow and tomorrow are as these — the seventh
spreading itself: an animal almost still.

There is a darkness here, one I am familiar with.
Yet it comes inside as if it were the first time: slowly,
watching the eyes. I entered a woman once like this —
at Christmas, her parents shopping. Hearing them
in the garage we hurried upstairs; saw her father
with the small body — the squirrel — holding it,

stroking cold. It was a gift from a previous summer.
I recall how she stood naming it, cradling newspaper
until I took it away, the cheap gray staying.

I am reminded by all things of that which is left.
By fragments and by feel I piece it back.
It is this hard to dream. After sleep I rise,
dress in brown, sleeves surrounding me.
It is a good fit.

The Barkers

1
Good days, we are what we have at hand—
a house, land, tickets to a carnival.
The first time I met Mrs. Dailey she said,
"Hi. I'm Mrs. Dailey. I have cancer,"
and sat on the porch nodding
while her husband screamed at me
for cutting weeds away from their house.

That night the wind blew a scent of coal smoke,
crying of an old woman rocking by a window,
stopping to shout: "Where's my pill, Poppa?
He's cut my flowers."

2
You smell sawdust, lean over the rail,
miss twice, three times.
"Try again," he tells you. But the bottles stay put.
In the booth beside you someone drops the Bozo.
You hear him hit, hear the water and words,
the cussing. You move on.

Everywhere the lights, crowds—cotton-candy,
snowcones—the mothers dragging sons
dragging dogs.
At the next booth you are breaking balloons.
The barker will tell you to leave
when you begin winning:
"One prize," he will say, his best W. C. Fields.

Nearby, there is a woman —
young and tough, a dyed blonde.
The lights turn her hair as she steps forward.
She does Mae West.
The woman you want to know,
want to take home, sleep with,
make fun of her three-for-a-quarter line,
tell her how when it is over
you expect one bright light,
sweeping across all you have ever done.
Coming to a stop on this small
stuffed dog she's let you win.

3
Tonight they auctioned Fred Dailey's household goods,
his hammers and a chain saw I could have bought.
It took less than six hours.
The kids played on the old porch
and on the hedge between our houses.
Fred would have hated it,
would have called those small bodies sons-a-bitches.
Spit tobacco through his teeth,
been annoyed by the banter of bidding,
voice of the auctioneer,
the spotlight they used at dark
that made everything seem old and cheap.

Blue Pony Rag

Fat man in Navy whites holds with both hands
the steel through the middle of a blue pony.
Face and body blur, go by
braced for that sudden stop.
Nearby, dragonfly lands on a row of prizes,
tests the eye of a stuffed bear,
small boy pointing to a statue of Charlie McCarthy.

The man in the booth lights a cigarette,
blows smoke in the face of the child,
then motions him back with a cane.
A father's big arm comes from nowhere,
grabs the barker, his hand,
crushes all five fingers.

The dragonfly rises.
On the carousel, sailor looks once
then to the docks,
slap of water loud by the bumper cars.

The New Air Force Tucks Itself in Minutes from the Alamo

for Scott and Nate

When Jim Smallwood knelt on his bunk
at Lackland Air Force Base
and gently parted the air in a demonstration
of oral sex, he had no idea
Master Sergeant Walter T. Bare
was standing in the shadows.
Neither did we.
The whole barracks watched as Smallwood
inserted his tongue, two fingers.
After eight weeks of Basic Training,
all we had was thin air
and Jim Smallwood who did everything but moan.

Finally, Sgt. Bare stepped forward.
Everyone but Smallwood saw him, arms folded,
a look in his eyes like maybe anything could happen
and would if he said so.
The instant Smallwood turned around
opened like the air he'd shown us.
When Bare smiled, you knew there was a God
and He knew where Texas was
and didn't mind a little fun in the hour before bed.

They Always Bloom

The November it takes dozens of passes
to cut through and mine the shallow vein,
something in the muscle resists to the last cell,
holds stubborn as late corn east Illinois snow fence,
holding, giving and holding.

"Paperwhite narcissus for indoor forcing," the ad says.
Clear white flowers on graceful stems.
Exhibition grade. Fragrance that permeates a room
two full weeks. $23.00 postpaid.
I buy them for the barracks, for the guarantee.
They hesitate and each gray day
prove right Sgt. Cicero Taylor who says,
"Nothing grows here. Nothing white."

Stitches tight at my wrist, I water and coax
and hope-cover. When one finally does come up,
it is with a wariness, tentative shoot
halved again, the greater hunger
sore above all this waste and winter at the glass.

Barracks

1
When they brought Jack Parrish back the third time
he had tears in his eyes,
both wrists bandaged where the metal of the cuffs
had dug in.
He dropped down heavy on the bed,
rubbed his arm, recalling
how they dragged him kicking, from the waterfront,
beat him three flights up from the hold of a ship.
I offer him a cigarette.
"Had it made," he says, pack-tapping it tight.
I sit taking it in,
hearing Jack inhale, breathe out,
smoke rising, thinning
like the sound a mattress makes,
springs yielding to the weight of this or any man.

2
The room I share with him is small.
The door, left open, leaves it seeming larger.
"Fuck This Shit," is carved in the wall above my bed.
I lie on my back, reading the last thirty years,
fall asleep, still in uniform,
and Jack, entering, wakes me.

He does not mention last winter when I slit my wrist,
circled, in blood, the words on the wall,
says nothing of his father's suicide.
He has a new girl, comes in dancing,
naked to the waist, singing Sinatra.
That night as we lie talking,
he tells me he is afraid for his mother,
being beaten by a man she is afraid to leave.

37

"I try to have faith," he says. "I pray."
In a week he would strangle on his own vomit,
the only casualty of a party in Parrish Hall—
I swear to God.

3
A year after Parrish I am out.
The day I sign the papers the sun is shining.
Five hours later, bus leaving Rantoul,
it begins to rain.
A girl in the street waves to me
from under her umbrella. In Columbus,
a cab driver shatters that, tries to make me.
4 A.M., High Street in the rain, I almost let him.
Then I remember the words above my bed,
get out at the light.

Soldier

Forty years after, Arthur Dixon dreams
of Luzon, of friends heart-shot at arm's length.
He talks of the war in the Pacific often
and at inappropriate times, in church
confuses salvation
with the final victory on New Guinea.

Husks of Viceroy smoke wreathe over a table.
Crenellated drape hems hang gray, hang
and bounce against a sill.
He sits all day by the window, at evening
unfolds a small Japanese flag.
They came at us, thousands of them.
They were screaming. When it was over
we counted them, went through pockets.
I forget how many.
They told us to look for maps.
We saw their children's pictures.

The dull drapes brush the duller sill,
almost touch it, touch it then billow.
There is enough pain in this man
that you look hourly for some spark of redemption
to open or blaze, even for an instant.
His plaintive arguing toward hope
draws you in, breaks you,
fixes the animal cadence
and the voice is both your voices.

Once, between these indifferent walls,
Peggy Potter Ramsdail laid on hands
and cured a migraine. Now the lath
will not accept a nail without profanity.
The whole bruised house conspires, old pine
inching off-square the way the Lost, he imagines,
advance after death, unhurried in the dark.

Arcana

A divine nimbus exhales from it
from head to foot . . .
Hair, bosom, hips, bend of legs,
negligent falling hands all diffused.
—Walt Whitman

The spring Butch Thompson and I
rented a trailer in Rantoul, Illinois,
the sun rose each morning
through a diamond-shaped
window on the wood door.
Within a week of moving in,
Butch had covered the diamond
with a poster of Tina Turner.
First light began between her thighs.
I never want to forget that.

I move tonight in borrowed clothes, my uncle's,
his good scent flown with any clear memory of him.
Four years after his death
I can muster only that ecstatic look
at a discussion of freemasonry,
every handshake and shibboleth gone up
like kindling.
In the stove, dry-stacked maple and birch bark,
striate and smooth, burns and down.
Changed air hurries against the cold.

It is a poor soldiery marks our going,
and little calls us back.
Consider the night Walt Whitman met with
Secretary of the Treasury Salmon P. Chase,
Republican from Ohio, to discuss a possible clerkship.
Consider how Whitman held in his hand
a signed letter from Ralph Waldo Emerson;
how Chase did not sing the body electric;
how the Secretary of the Treasury
dreamed of the Presidency after Lincoln;
how he collected signatures.
Consider Whitman speaking eloquently
of the Union dead,
of the necessity of not forgetting,
while Chase mentally positioned the framed
Emerson on the wall between Longfellow
and Francis Scott Key.
Consider Butch Thompson, sunrise
on South Chanute Street,
all that blazing symmetry and a brand new day.

Upon Trying the Door
of Mark Twain's House

1
At 17, the road to Hannibal, Missouri,
is hours of corn- and beanfield—
honeysuckled barnsides,
clear May sky the only limit.
Three days a runaway, I stand finally
before the white two-story, corner drainspout
smooth with down-sliding at midnight.
"After five," a caretaker apologizes,
leaves me to look in lower floor windows.

When I have seen enough—Hill Street
and the famous fence, tea roses in bloom—
I walk to Becky Thatcher's Bookstore,
steal a copy of *Life on the Mississippi*.
Outside, beyond Mark Twain Savings & Loan,
noise of men drunk as boys, side-arming stones
into water part Wapsipinicon, part the Des Moines.

2
My uncle, William Barnett, wears a hat like Bogart—
big-brimmed, the kind that hides thinning hair.
This morning he buries a brother-in-law.
Outside Banks and Craft Funeral Home, under eaves
as rain pours down,
I want him to tell me about the time
he went for a loaf of bread, joined the Navy.
How it was he neglected to tell them
he had four children, a wife; later
how he got Blanche to see the recruiter.
Lady, don't you s'pose he knew he had them kids?

In the haze of this played-out town
he says only, "Gonna be a bitch, that hill.
Was with Earl." As always the dread comes first—
twenty years, mornings going from light
into the close dark of mines
that cross Whitesburg, Fleming-Neon even now.
First the dread, then God only knows.
We do well not to send him after bread.

The L & K Plays Host to the Class of '72

In a restaurant off Hebron Road,
between the Sohio and Doc Gutridge's place,
we drank Cokes one summer and talked to death
the few dreams Heath, Ohio, had its hands on.
Rod Slonaker, Jerry Peters. We would pull in.
Mike Yoder, Ed Laurenzo. Seven, seven-thirty.
Jon Landrum, Mark Chapman. And order and talk
till they locked the doors around ten.
Dave Hanley, Tom Kozlowski.
Ice water and air-conditioning
that June, July, and August.
I remember most the air at night, still hot,
smell from the one refinery and how it
nudged us in our places there
between Ramp Creek and the Licking River.
Even the dogs at Doc Gutridge's wanted to wake us.
The song that year was "Anticipation." A8.
Pushed till the buttons stayed.
In the parking lot, on Mark Chapman's Ford,
we counted change—
how many quarts of three-two beer
we had between us. Into the light came Camaros.
JoAnn Clutter, April Fisher. Idling, numinous.
Diane Harkness, Sherry Link. Wide-eyed.
Beth MacDonald, Betty Seamen.
Bright as every wish that fell from fenders,
from three-inch speakers, the same one song.

The Importance of Singing Before Long Silence

Think of the surprise—iris of rope
closing like a fist, pine rafter refusing to give.
Think of the pain blossoming
as you step from the body, all that weight,
test of bone you had no intention of testing.
Think of the view: rising now,
looking back at a dark
that is all this and swallows it whole.
After, not a word.

Call it perfection.
Yet the air here sleeps too soundly.
You look down upon a last spark
indrawn because not one new tree or cotyledon
in this great spring shakes at your going.
Not one.
Still, in the morning, a mother will scream
and lift with all that is in her.

When they have cut you down,
she alone recalls the bath—wood squares
floating red and blue,
rectangle sailing the coast of a leg.
You are hardly marked.
A dry mouth hangs open.
And they will break both jaws before the day is out
to close you.

Poem for Walter Tevis

What I hear in the night I subtract from to name.
Scrimmage of cricket and diesel singing,
pulse and absence of pulse. In the lindens,

branches flex, hold,
hold inabsolute and declare.

The little halves made of this
redivide until, small and still,
they are every uttered word, insatiate,

hard-praying we forget speech,
that a man has died and young.

What I say aloud
somersaults off house-wood and highway,
off whatever light or gray squirrel

descends articulate, at least one god in hearing.

The Chillicothe Oaks Talk of Tecumseh

for Elaine Dabelko

Moneto had His hands on you.
That night by the fire you spoke quietly
to eight braves who listened as you rose
and in one motion smothered suddenly
the light thirty white men steered by.
Freed, you circled back and leaped in faces
that knew you as Death's brother at least,
your tomahawk a long time moving.
Your brother Chiksika said then you would lead,
said he would be shot between the eyes,
the enemy at a great distance.
When it came, you caught his body,
rode slowly back in the Hunger Moon.

At fifteen you had asked, Why not one nation?
At forty leaned by one of us, leaned down
and kissed John Galloway's daughter — once
on each eye, then full on the mouth.
By the Scioto that night, she said she would
marry you. If you lived white.
When you left her, you knew it was coming.
A drawing of blood. Seneca Oneida Mohawk Ottawa
Wyandot Winnebago moving and convinced
as the day the eclipse came, came as you said,
every stirred leaf agreeing you were born to this.

48

After the betrayal, at the last battle,
you predicted your death, gave an iron rod:
When you see me fall, fight your way to my side.
Strike my body four times.
I will then arise and lead you to victory.
You knew then it was over, saw as we did
Wasegoboah running for you, fullspeed and falling.
Saw them come and lift and lay you under one of us,
small truth above the breast blue-dark in the little light.

The Fire in Earnest

The Moving Arm of God, it has been said,
can be seen in a wave at sea, in routed armies.
I see it the moment I close the door to Sandy Lee's
Camaro—blonde hair against the gray of the seat,
the way she rushes lights.
Could've been Thomas Edison, I consider as she drives.
Ablaze and 33 in 1880, phonograph to my credit,
meeting Sarah Bernhardt. After dinner,
lighting December Menlo Park a first time
for this actress; explaining incandescence,
the body invention enough.
On leaving she'd compare me to Napoleon—
relentless—
on the stairs, lean to be kissed.

Sandy Lee's new Camaro denies years muscle
between us.
I take her hand.
It is not Menlo Park, 1880, but Columbus, Ohio,
that time before sunset when, walking,
circles of street coins find us, leap up perfect almost.
On the radio: *Young faces grow sad and old,*
hearts of fire grow cold. We know that.
Three questionable lights, answered kiss
at Broad and High.
What we don't know is when.

Certain Flowers Persist

1
To feed the robins
and redbirds of southeast Ohio
you feed a few crows.
Dark and loud above yesterday's bread,
they strut the edge of a cistern top.
Light on their feet,
never long in one place, they remind me
of the night I said simply:
Mommy, can we see that woman with the kayak again?
Snow falling straight near the eave
rises and breaks
smooth as the lie my father told to cover himself:
Would I do that and take him with me?
Another gust and bread
collects above the cistern, half-circles upward.
What woman?
A last crow stands eyeing crust.
By fence, slow cat stretches.
What kayak?

2
By the time I could spell *gasoline*
it had become the one thing that reminded me
of my father.
Somehow the cigarettes and Old Spice
never quite overcame it.
Twenty years later, there is so much
I could do without—
memory of how he left,
Sundays before that, riding the tank of his Harley
out Wilmington Pike.
Back roads past the station he owned,
beyond the filled parking lots of churches,
into Kettering from the Greene County side:
hands over his on the grips, head high,
hair cut like his.
Because he took me with him
more than once
before finally standing in the living room
of the house on Comanche Drive,
hugging my mother whom he had just divorced.
Because he took me with him
I forgave the time I called him all day,
his saying he would be right there,
that he never came.
Because he took me with him
I read to my son as if there were no such time.
Head on my chest, he listens,
closes the book, holds out a hand
and says the two words he knows best: *ice cream.*
Suddenly it is Sunday.
I am flying past fields,
noise of tractor loud as locusts.
And always the smell from hands, brown
uniform shirt reading *Roy's Shell.*

3
By the Chesapeake & Ohio line
outside of Nelsonville, honeysuckle grows
as if spilled coal and rust were heaven on earth.
Certain flowers persist.
Even in winter they will not let go.
Like the hundreds of thousands who exist
day to day,
these vine roots have a sense there is water,
and if water, reason to grow.
Each spring those who walk here
choose between the short stride of railbed,
the grab and tangle of that which will not be moved.
You can tell newcomers by the black knees
of their pants, cinder burns,
the quick curse they have for honeysuckle.

III

The Heart as Second Child

The heart wakes
suddenly
alert, at the foot of their bed.
                    —Suzanne Cleary

She has painted one breast black
and hid the other. Nothing works.
It does what it wants—talks early,
rolls from every counter and couch,

refuses to crawl.

She puts it in the low wicker swing
beside ponies, chromatic leaves
blowing, pennantlike.

The ponies move from shade.
End-chains of the swing rock, arhythmic.

She sits, lifts the loose blouse
and smiles, small of shoulder,
the world without her
cow's milk and rice, difficult to down.

She fears this one may never wean.
Always by the ponies, the brook,
transfixed,
prisoner to that accustomed rushing.

Mario Soto Drops His Head in Disappointment as George Hendrick Circles the Bases

In 1984, I was one out and one strike away
from a no-hitter against the Cards.
On the 2-2 count, I took a chance—
nervous as I was—and threw a change-up.
They said he struck it in the green seats, left-center.
I knew when I threw it, that pitch was trouble.
And I hung it.
And George was looking for it.

Hell, in the seventh, the second baseman
had to barehand one and shovel it to Driessen
at first to just nip the runner.
After that though, I thought it was in the books.
Couple of years before in New York,
pitching against the Mets,
we were ahead 3-1 in the ninth.
Kingman came up and he had been
killing my change-up all night.
I threw him one and he killed it.
Tied the game. Same goddamn pitch.
If George Hendrick is up again in that situation,
I'm going to bounce him four balls.
Bounce those babies so high
he'll have to buy box seats to swing at 'em.
Next time.

Physical Science

All I know about you, dark-haired Wes Williams,
is that you quarterbacked
the high school varsity squad
two seasons and stepped down your senior year,
something unheard of,
that you wrote poetry beside me the hour a day
I listened to physics lectures,
heard how, in 1911, physicist Ernest Rutherford
said the atom is a central positive nucleus
with negative electrons moving at an outer influence.
Rutherford's atom *should* collapse, Wes. Remember?
Equal but oppositely charged particles
colliding entropically inward. It doesn't.
And doesn't often enough that we exist,
accommodating inlets of light and probability.

The day you pushed the ledger you wrote in
my way, I felt a pull.
No outside agency pushes the electron, and no
internal clockwork times the jump.
It just happens, for no particular reason,
now rather than then.
The last time I saw you, you were playing pinball:
SU chatter ring flip P flip ER
twenty thousand bonus flip
MA ring flip N flip drain.
SAME PLAYER SHOOTS AGAIN glowing
under Lois Lane.

We have to interfere with the processes
in order to observe them at all.
I laid a quarter on the glass.
You played it without looking up.
I don't think you knew or cared that I'd
begun to write myself and was waiting to thank you.
Now I hear you've given it up, burned everything.

Tonight Wes, there's a fire under the moon.
Four horses huddle at its edge in the cold.
The stoop-shouldered man must have a reason
to pile on so much this late,
to toss the dark wood in and whole.

"And Clear Dances Done in the Sight of Heaven"

1

They don't say it but move as if steel were spirit,
something near and sure, worth fearing
as it settles in, foot by foot, pure event.
At each incantatory joining,
bolt and temporary bolt, the old tonality
of beginning and again beginning.
This, the idealism welded into days and weeks,
comes forward in the act of walking high iron
to paint the last beam white
and ride the one elevator forty stories down,
recalling the leather and how it held in ice
and wind, against that goddamn-it-to-hell
once or twice you come back from
if you're sharp and watching.
This ride they shake from them
the feel of three-and-a-half-inch-wide wing iron
strolled easy as sidewalk.
Beyond, the Cuyahoga catches what light it can.
Light in summer here gold and close
its last hour, going from the ground up,
in no hurry.

2

The year Dallas won the Super Bowl on a Hail Mary,
hard work came down to Drew Pearson's hands
and could he hold it once it was there.
Staubach knew when he tossed that 80-yarder.
He followed through with his whole body.
The first time I fought
there exploded a sense of celebration
not unlike that catch.
A fine spark stayed in the eyes years after.
The night Keith Rhodes covered my blind side
in a jazz bar in Athens, Ohio —
three good-sized men waiting a clear shot —
the spark was enough. When they had gone,
we drank straight whiskey
and mourned the chance
to risk it, bare knuckled and back to back.

Lately, moving is lay-ups that land clean.
Half-court shots that score, all net,
or float that blessed extra inch.
Jim Wallace. Bill Toth can tell you
it is an edge that comes and goes
like sweat or soreness in a shoulder.
After, in the shower,
you recall the pass, see an arm up-curving,
the shot on its way. On the rim,
two points down, you hear again
the difference between want and need,
single *son-of-a-bitch* as the ball circles, considers,
considers, then drops.
The heart and lungs know this is what we come for.
Fair fight and rush of blood, the blocked jumper
underneath. Still, some days the moves leave
and you reach up like Bill Toth, say *No, by God*
and get your own rebound.
Do that for twenty years, you've got something.

The One Good Reason Becomes Apparent

A blind horse wades by feel,
Reaches a fence of wire and pine
Dividing a pool, shallow line between rivals.
Another stallion, years younger,
Swims into and under the wire, eases
Instinctively into the area
Where the blind one flexes old shoulders.
Biting, rearing to wound,
Mouths open, close around neck flesh.
From water, manes streaming,
Legs stumble, let go.
Long pieces of lodgepole pine bend then break.
Wood passes into horse.
One heart, bursting, sprays ground
That will take hours to dry black.
The other stallion watches the mares, unmoved.

A V of geese breaks above, neutral music
Played and gone to noise.
They travel this way, in simple halves,
Not for beauty's sake,
Not the least awed by evening or other geese
Or air at sunset, seed-heavy
And every bit as north- as south-going.
They travel and recall not one sore wing.
What they do in light and after is fill the sky.

Moving the River

At a wide walk this morning the Hocking
stepped its way south,
one syllable shy its other name, *Hockhocking.*
Delaware for "bottleneck."
Predictability the aim and rule, how
do you move a river?
Ask the Army Corps of Engineers
who straightened in a year
the slow curving of ten thousand.
In the Radiation Department, University Hospital,
they use lollipops in the shape of hens
to coax reluctant ones. My sister, too old for that,
goes because, simply, it is life
and we are such a long time dead.

The day Mario Soto drew his second fine
and suspension of the '84 season,
I took her to a treatment. Lymph cancer.
Two- and three-year-olds compared target markings,
indelible dot-lines on foreheads, on necks.
To keep from staring, I thought of you, Mario.
Untamed. That particular Reds-Braves game.
Tell it straight: when Claudell Washington
tossed that bat and came after you in Atlanta,
you wanted a piece of him.
At Wrigley a week before, you'd erupted
at Ron Cey's homer,
the hit clearly two feet foul. All or none,
both dugouts emptying,
you nudged an umpire who reversed the call.
Such spirit. Like a Mantle or Rose.
Nine innings, total war.

By this river, I dream we are right, fair,
and win because we are,
that the stars, old gods, go with us.
Great turned sycamores regarding the act not at all,
a woman strips cattails,
child running, arms out in the seed down.

Independence Day

Once a year we send up what has gone before
the way ash at the edge of a leaf
rises to wind, all at once.
Columns of sparks not quite cold
flow onto hollyhock and ivy.
A child suggests they are hurting God.

Edna Carpenter, 80 this month,
knots a cotton rag to the window
of her house on the ridge above town.
She is letting her one neighbor know
she is all right. Down the hill,

in sand beside grandchildren,
inch-high dinosaur rears an oblong head,
teeth bared, tongue upward at invisible fruit.
All this as in ice, great pterodactyl jaws
still and open. By the slide
toy backhoe and dozer
dream of roads, new republics even here.

Ralph Waldo Emerson Addresses the ICBM Silos at Minot, North Dakota

Great power, it would seem, does not make us happy.
Nature herself in full voice cries out:
In the wild turmoil
Thou ridest to power / And to endurance.
Endurance, not negation.
Is this what Liberty has come to?
Even Freedom, Democracy?
The defense of an idea cannot risk futures
it has no claim to.
On such a subject eloquence is easy:
The State is a poor, good beast who means the best;
it means friendly. A poor cow who does well by you —
do not grudge it its hay. It cannot eat bread,
as you can; let it have without grudge
a little grass for its four stomachs.
You, who are a man walking cleanly on two feet,
will not pick a quarrel with a poor cow.
Take this handful of clover and welcome.
But if you hook me when I walk in the fields,
then, poor cow, I will cut your throat.

"The cost of a thing is the amount
of what I will call life
required to be exchanged for it."
In defending Liberty as you do, you risk forever
that incandescent Once. Were it my time
I would walk from it, outgrow the Poor Cow.
In my time you died singly.
Even at Gettysburg, five-deep, they knew

67

eventually birds would sing,
good rain have its full say.
In Concord in those days, huckleberries
bloomed in perennial heat, promise of hot cobbler
to show for an ache in the small of the back.
Today, Mennonite aprons empty, fill and empty.
Young copperheads sun in plain sight.

In the Shelter

When it happened, we prayed and went,
dread air coming even as we moved.
The few who will and choose
go up now and forage and burn the dead.

Tonight the first snow since
melts over linden and pine root,
rough circle of grasses
showing apocryphal and small,
monochrome stubble of moonlight holding entirely.

A good hour, we hand them in.
Soul and all. *If I had*
A hundred tongues, a hundred mouths, a voice
Of iron, I could not tell of all the shapes.

George Balanchine's Cat Commemorates the 37th Anniversary of the Normandy Invasion

> For he will not do destruction if he is well-fed,
> neither will he spit without provocation.
> —Christopher Smart

The yellow-white Tabby is too much present,
like correspondents who came ashore
unarmed, explaining the hedgerows
and soft undersides of tanks,
their work to make sense of this much death.
The simple business of Balanchine's cat
to fly backward, proud-eyed.

Like Stravinsky, she loves to eat.
Like Baryshnikov, is one of a kind—
leaps, turns twice in midair
as if gravity were hearsay.

That last-second catch pulls together cat limbs
the way the first wave of Rangers, one body,
pulled together climbing the great cliffs:
ladders of rope, a terrible rain
over all their nine lives.

Now she slide-steps through a living room
laden with Pollocks, paint lines coiling like wire.
Now, the same old arching of the spine,
every inch world war.
Like this they must have waded in and in.
Because the sea would not hold, the tide kept coming.

The Blue Monkey's Dream of Shore

We called it living dangerously,
those walks along north-south tracks, naming flowers.
Phlox, beardtongue, onion.
The same thirty or forty kinds grow this year,
though without a faith that anything can happen.
Nights I wake now in panic, both hemispheres
of the brain believe the worst:
I have wandered onto ice
and inch across its thin face, a bruise
it would be done with. Beside me,
small blue monkey shivers, blows on its hands.
The ice breaks around us.
"Swim for it," she says in perfect English.

Why I am the last to know the clear earth is going,
I have no idea.
There is in me a habit of half seeing.
Were it sickness and not habit,
I could sever what is sick.
Were it sleep, I could wake in part.
On their own, the eyes know a whole dark lake,
heart-curve of moon, how
once in the water
there is little not ballast for this chill swim.

All the way, she holds to me and I to her.
Somewhere an entire orchestra plays
as, onshore, we shake ourselves.
The blue monkey is inclined at once farther inland.
When she is gone, a scent of olives
follows every move.

71

On the Failure of All Political Poems

Out here, finding water is first work.
Fire follows. A newspaper by last light.
A world away, the *New Jersey*
shells Shiite positions in the hills around Beirut.
In the city, as Neruda said,
the blood of children flows through the streets,
easy, as the blood of children will do.

Holes bullets open in bodies, no words close.
Journalists know this,
know how impotent and hollow air is
the second before impact. In a photograph,
twin belts of ammunition cross the militiaman's chest
for just this reason.

Here, in the loud silence of wilderness,
beside a man I can trust with my life,
I bury wood still burning.
Fine smoke rises from the loose earth.
After, under blankets,
I count stars, thankful the dark has its limits.
We number them all the way to sleep, these stars,
hear, high in Douglas fir, one owl
who will get no water, not a drop this far in.

Turning Thirty the Year Orwell Made Famous

1
In one of those new thin-walled theatres,
Debra Winger dying on the third of four screens,
sound to *Snow White* bleeding through,
I grieve a death years translate to small fictions.
What is this sickness that radiates
nothing past the self?
Nothing that does not cleave and dissipate?
Hi-ho, hi-ho,
it's home from work we go.
As if a kiss could come in time
and fan a heat we circle round:
Her lips blood red, her hair like night.
It's fitting the astronaut in the Winger film
tells of hurtling from that great height,
the only sound crossing to dark
a determined heartbeat.

The man I mourn too late and badly
would have had no use for the astronaut-Nicholson.
That killer smile constricting slightly,
telling volumes on us.
He believed in grace. The forgiveness kind.
The day I fed him, the fact he hated cooked carrots
kept him going enough to reach for ice cream
he said tasted like paper.
I think sometimes the embarrassment at the end
killed him—the having to be fed
and shaved and turned
in the white bed off the hall
where those who could shuffled yet the close step.

73

I've watched the husk-sleep close
and wished it had not (wished it then),
wished it were the sleep of film.
Snow White risen, kissed and singing.
Now, that wish and Jack Nicholson's smile
go up and out. No holding them.
Nothing to be done but turn and wish again.
Wish and smile. *Little something I picked up*
out in space.

2
In the air above Angel Ridge,
there is a hard cold
as if it were not all downhill from here,
sumac bright as flame
and every third oak shoot sure to last.
Same cold that brings the breath in clouds
turns gray and easy spent as dimes
from a railroad bridge, wishes bigger than all Ohio.
Could I wish it, I would slow the rush,
look back into a valley
climbed from because there is time.
Yet to come this way is to come knowing
night is sudden here, the berries of the sumac
edible a week at most.
No amount of wishing changes fact.
Still, this is the place to lean against a deer-rub
and laugh and turn thirty.
Lantern below on the road lighting pine tassels,
big maple brown with drought, fir needles
the nearest green and that going.

Autumn, Coffman's Farm

West-facing old roof stares at sunset,
one corner open to pin oak and tulip leaves
settling through bare 4 × 8's.
The fat groundhog I frighten taking stock
knows I've no business here,
that the pens inside have been empty
of cattle and horse all his short life.

Any weekend I can drive the hour north
and walk this place a block from where my father
and mother eat, sleep and rise
to work the years to retirement.
This fall I have come twice
to stumble the face of field gone to its own,
to mourn and praise a brevity
this barn both affirms and contradicts.

How little what-we-live-by-and-never-see changes,
how slow and then at once:
this year half the overhang, the year before
a sandstone footer, in one place letting go.
Still, lightning rods rest obvious atop the tin,
rust-dull, five equidistant fingers
remembering to reach and why.

For Matthew

1
He cries so close to me,
the sound something between a breath
and breathing scared;
into my shoulder, the skin,
as if this were the place to put such things.

Soon, his mother is beside us singing.
But the crying keeps up
until his mouth is full of her.
She holds him,
his cheeks indrawn, sucking,
seeing, behind eyes,
that spark of recognition we cannot get enough of.

After he has eaten, is sleeping,
I carry him down the hall
to the bed my mother gave him.
Here, he will sleep, wake,
wonder at the quiet creaking beneath him,
bed rocking as he kicks.

2
The last of the clowns spins above,
turning its one string to a stop.
On his back he watches,
and when the hands are there, around him,
tenses, eyes wide,
as if this were too much too soon.

Yet the touch is something so expectedly sure
he follows it through air
to where it brings to his mouth
a sweetness wet and new, taste so special
he will recall it long after this lifting.

Neon

It's not nostalgia to be going home,
stairs steeper this trip, stopping once
halfway up and again at the top.
Your grandson, a step lower,
holding a bag of army men,
polite as you introduce him.
You could of rung, Aunt Frances; I'd come got this —
niece carrying all you own
apart from land you've come to sell.
In the room: *I'm too old for this, Hazel.*

She knows why you tell her, knows you know
the Bentleys own this town, Bentley Hotel,
where the boy at your feet — a Bentley —
tears into the pack of soldiers with his teeth,
spills them predictably over the dark floor.
That evening on the television,
his heroes smile fire and sword
and ride bareback the road from Rome,
forward world picking up speed.
In the movie, the poet Antoninus
comes to the camp of the gladiator
knowing sleight of hand, how to sing.
Spartacus, tired of the fight, tells him
to say again the song that ends *I look home.*
At the end, in chains, Antoninus asks,
"Could we have won? Could we ever have won?"

78

In the featherbed, after praying,
you tell the boy
in the sad voice you wear more and more
of his uncles, Ed and Earl Potter,
shot on separate occasions just up the street.
You forget, in the dark, you are telling a child,
recall a detail that will not let him sleep.
Like the week you said every act is life and death
and he braked the whole way,
red two-wheeler carrying him irrevocably down,
sidewalk seams clicking front tire
back tire to the point of singing.

Fish Kite

I slept so easily then.
On the hard pressboard of a stockroom bench,
coarse uniform coat folded as pillow,
steady hydraulic drone and hiss in the lift bay.
Heavy doors up and down, big V-8s catching,
pump bell sounding and constant.
I could sleep through all that, eight years old
and dreaming of dragons whose terrible surfacings
I carried like string. The quiet always woke me,
my father counting cash and checks,
mentally dissecting the hemi-stock Plymouth
he ran Sundays at a drag strip near Xenia.
Day's end, we'd ride his XKE down Wilmington Pike,
racing Ivan Taylor to the raised bridge on Woodman
where the Jaguar, complaining,
flew those long seconds into summer.
The night neither my father nor Ivan would yield
at the place the bridge narrowed,
they touched doors, airborne.
We played a game at the station
where the Coke bottle with the stamped city
farthest from Dayton won.
It wasn't so much the distance
as the way you got to smile and say *Phoenix
Houston Seattle* and feel that firm pat
on the shoulder or back.

Today, the bundled boy pays out string,
indigo and gold billowing
taut fin and gill and sunlight in pockets.
At the fence, looped twine tight to his hand,
he scissor-steps, stares vertically —
If I let go now — then runs
unmired across stubble and furrow,
chill morning smelling of leaf-mold.
In the upper currents, the fish sleeve
undulates, at its zenith
eating downdrafts that turn and eddy
abundantly. I do not know his name,
or care as he moves from me,
holding yet the thin filament, here to there.

Collecting

For twenty years now my father has repaired
guidance systems. He does a good job
and is well paid.
Portions of his work collect in various Minuteman
and Trident missiles aimed anonymously at millions.
The summer I worked there, third shift,
I watched him mornings through the gates
to the last guard
and saw it could make perfect sense
moving like this, with the others.
To the drum-taps prompt,
The young men falling in and arming.
I could move like that.

Or like Joe Martelle, clamming the upper Mississippi,
carrying a crowfoot bar to his johnboat
the spring I was born. In a photograph, out at dawn:
"Look at them hooks and all that heavy chain.
What if I was out here alone and snagged my coat
when I dropped that bar into the river?"
Inscription at the bottom of the old Kodak:
Joe had been on the Mississippi a long time
and hadn't drowned so far.
I could move like that, sun at my back
and feeding the big Lab pup beside me in the boat
mussel meat, hailing John Peacock, pearl buyer,
as he waves from his place beyond the reeds.

I have a choice to make
and so imagine Joe Martelle, drowned,
still peripheries and the good wave we make
going down: johnboat adrift, black dog
at the dead helm staring to shore and back forever.
It doesn't help. Always at last I see
my father, intent and working in close
as if our lives and his rose in the blue solder smoke.

Ballooning

I have felt the wind of the wing of madness
pass over me.

—Baudelaire

You've seen it before: the Blue Moon Bar & Grill,
Starlite Motel, the housing development
where 26 frontyard backyard fenced-yard worlds
overlap in summer light and dust, small boys
tending fire. Not one outrageous bird lands here.
All the dull colors nest in the trimmed trees.
Venation of the wickerwork nearby
crosses perfect lawns.

In these, we go where thinner air decides,
earth seeming to fall and silently.
Light in the hand acts this way,
warming, understaying its welcome
as if flying sunward something accrued.
Below, the sweet corn hot dog
elephant ear trailers
caravan I-71, Columbus to Cleveland,
boy in a truck reading *Mansfield Medina Akron.*

Tilt 'O Whirl and Wild Mouse quiet, I take her down.
Ticket halves blow by the hundreds
from the open bays of tractor trailers.
The boy in the truck waves aloft,
calls up George Kosta,
12 years old and the playground empty
the summer he announces
in his most grown-up voice,
Babies come out the ass. What he really wants
to swap the binoculars he watches Mrs. King with:
Natchrul blond. Takes these long baths.

84

There is power here
and close as the valve I open, grudgingly,
like the bidding that summer. Two Maris, two Mantle
and a Whitey Ford. *Throw in a Jim Bunning.*
A sucker for Bunning, George traded on the spot.
Every Tuesday through Sunday after, he'd laugh
and, reminding me what a good deal I'd gotten,
fill in — ankle to eye —
for the fact my bedroom window faced hillside.

From a height, it is easy to see
how we are confined — fence and highway, one life —
how a wave at God grounds us that still second
when all else fails,
and we fall in love with motion, any kind.

Mammalian Dive Reflex

for Lee Martin

I am in water and try to breathe.
A voice, words go up
to pull me across a still bay I know is sleep.
When I wake finally, I hold a live dog,
the feel of his dark back followed

like reef or coastline. There are questions
from a doctor who asks then repeats a name,
that I am safe and have survived
without air for forty minutes.

"This reflex," he says, "is just not present
after age ten. Not in humans."
My sister brings in photographs, the family Bible,
a book on seals that says what saved me
is common in the sea.

In each instance, the sudden slap of extreme cold
acts to shut down the animal's lungs.
A last surge of blood to the brain, however,
is key to survival. Some species
are thought to trigger the mechanism at will.

I dream my life all night for weeks
and fear the momentum, hearing in it
huge nothing. The dog, asleep, sighs loudly.
At my feet he is small and physical
and fills a white room just now with his noise.

"Keeping Their Difficult Balance"

1
The April morning Mike Yoder tells me
he is leaving the little church by Ramp Creek,
we skip rocks under the Route 79 Bridge.
He says he's taken up football, that girls
are interested if you make the team.
His sidearm that spring is amazing, first one
then another six-hopper up the center of the stream.

The long ones mean nothing now.
Started smoking too.
This from the kid who rides 30th Street
in the rain to sing and pray and drop
ten percent of his paper route into the offering.

The next Sunday, no Mike, I gather scrap wood
and make a kind of ship by lashing sticks
together with my good leather belt.
In the cooler air under the bridge, I push it out,
watch as it catches current, spins and sits,
a perfect target.

2
The good, small-town Ohio girls wouldn't
and so forced me to her,
old hardscrabble Latin body that opened
as she threw back thick hair, danced

wide circles in the bad light.
I know now she hated me, my not knowing,
gave me gonorrhea and a new name
to ease all that North American purity.

In the dank Airstream trailer by the tracks,
she spoke of home, two great rivers converging,
one repeated motion and afterward
the fine full curve, Meta become Orinoco.

3
This evening, me on the closest bench beside him,
my oldest digs and grades sand, builds
and levels and looks up, what he really wants
to wade the small creek near the park entrance
until his shoes are soaked, to pile and lay
flat stone so that either scant bank is his.

If there is a precipice, some dangerous
high place to stand and look down,
this must be it: heart-lungs
jetting faith and failed hope,
in equal measure,
oxygenated, toward every dark cell.
Hopewell Indians who buried dead here
knew there is mystery and connection, even in Ohio.

Ten, fifteen years ago
I did LSD here above acres of skull and rib
and femur. The world that night, the air,
hummed like a hit wiffle ball, hard-edged neon
of the Big Bear sign across the street
rearing, as now, incautiously at intervals till dawn.